For David, Laura, Garrett, Josh, Sam, Mom, and all the rescue cats we've loved!
With thanks to Hazel Hutchins and Alayne Kay Christian. – Dianna

Did you know?

Sometimes rescue cats need to be "socialized" before they can be adopted. This means they need to learn to interact with people without hissing, scratching, or biting. This behavior is usually caused by fear. The best way to socialize cats is to spend time with them, talking and playing.

Some rescue cats are feral, which means they have never lived with people. Other rescue cats may have gotten lost or been abandoned by their owners. It's important to remember that pets are part of the family!

Visit us on the Web at www.clavis-publishing.com.

James' Reading Rescue written by Dianna Wilson Sirkovsky and illustrated by Sara Casilda

ISBN 978-1-60537-611-0

This book was printed in June 2021 at Nikara, M. R. Štefánika 858/25, 963 01 Krupina, Slovakia.

First Edition
10 9 8 7 6 5 4 3 2 1

Clavis Publishing supports the First Amendment and celebrates the right to read.

Written by Dianna Wilson Sirkovsky
Illustrated by Sara Casilda

James' Reading Rescue

NEW YORK

What a horrible day!

Outside on the playground, James' friends whooped and hollered. Inside, James slumped at his desk, stumbling over words as he read aloud.

To cheer himself up, James stopped at the rescue shelter on the way home to visit the cat in the box. He'd named him **Ghost.**

James went straight to the box in the corner.
He crouched down to look inside. Green eyes stared back.

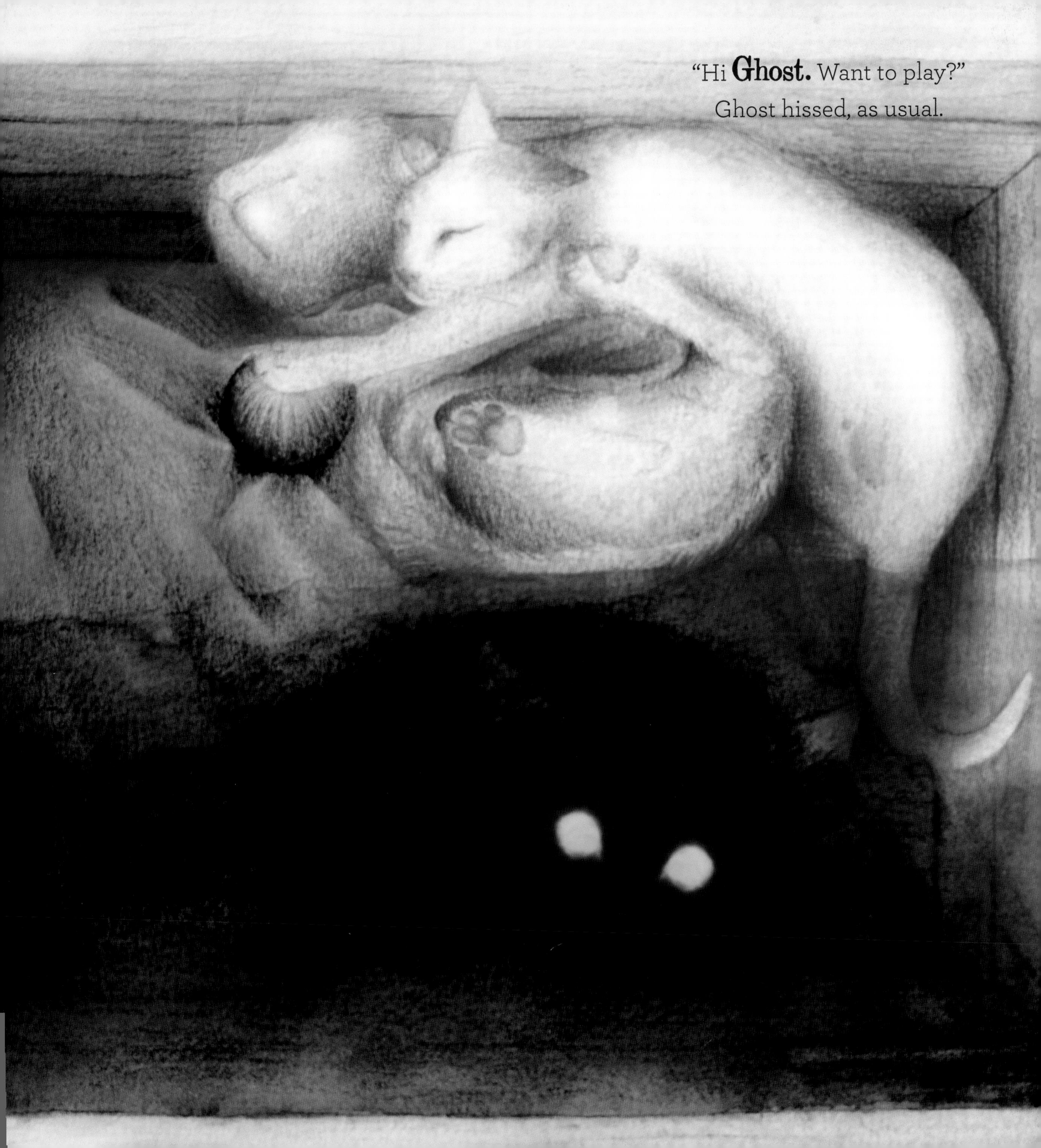

"Hi **Ghost.** Want to play?"

Ghost hissed, as usual.

James petted the friendlier cats.
He zigzagged around the room, dragging
a shoelace. Several cats chased it.

James flopped down beside the box and pulled a book from his backpack.
"I missed recess again," he said sadly. The cats made no comment.
"My teacher says I have to practice reading out loud."

He stumbled over words, but the cats didn't notice.
Some licked themselves. Some dozed.

Some listened.
Ghost was silent.

Weeks passed. Shelter cats came and went,
but **Ghost** remained crouched in his box as James
read and read. James was getting anxious.
What if no one adopted Ghost?

Every visit, James coaxed, “Ghost, come and play!”
He tried to tempt him with wind-up mice,
a feather duster, and even a laser dot to chase.
Ghost wouldn’t budge.

Maybe my stories aren't
exciting enough, James worried.
He ransacked the library.

"Here's *The Adventures of Sabretooth!*"
James snarled and growled through the story.
Ears and tails twitched.

When he finished,
James heard something
unexpected . . .

Purring from the box!

James read and read . . .
"Here's one just for you! *Ghost Cat's Haunted Halloween."*
James howled and yowled. **Ghost** purred.
Green eyes peered from the edge of the box.

"How about *Fast Freddy, the Commuter Cat?"*

Yeow.

James read and read until . . .

Ghost poked his head out of the box.

"Hello, Ghost," whispered James.

"Want to hear *The Amazing Ninja Cat?"*

Yeow.

James read and read until . . .
Ghost didn't hide in the box anymore.
Sometimes he sat on top. Sometimes he sat in front.
Always, his eyes were on James,
listening to every word.

Finally . . . one afternoon . . .
Ghost crept up beside him!
James slowly reached over and
stroked his fur for the first time.

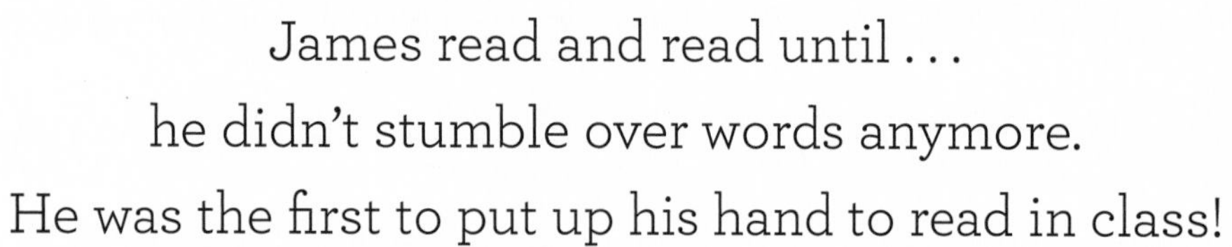

James read and read until . . .
he didn't stumble over words anymore.
He was the first to put up his hand to read in class!

And then one afternoon, the box wasn't in the corner. **Ghost** had been adopted! James grabbed his backpack and ran out. He knew he should be happy for Ghost, but he couldn't hide his tears.

He stumbled into his bedroom.
There was a box on his bed.
James lifted the lid and . . .

"Ghost!"

we're proud of you

James told his class about reading to **Ghost** and the shelter cats. Other children wanted to read to the cats too.

They practiced their reading, patiently listened to by cats who didn't judge. And the children loved the cats and helped them not to be afraid.

"Ghost," James murmured sleepily,
"you're the cat's meow."
Ghost rolled over and stretched.
Meow.

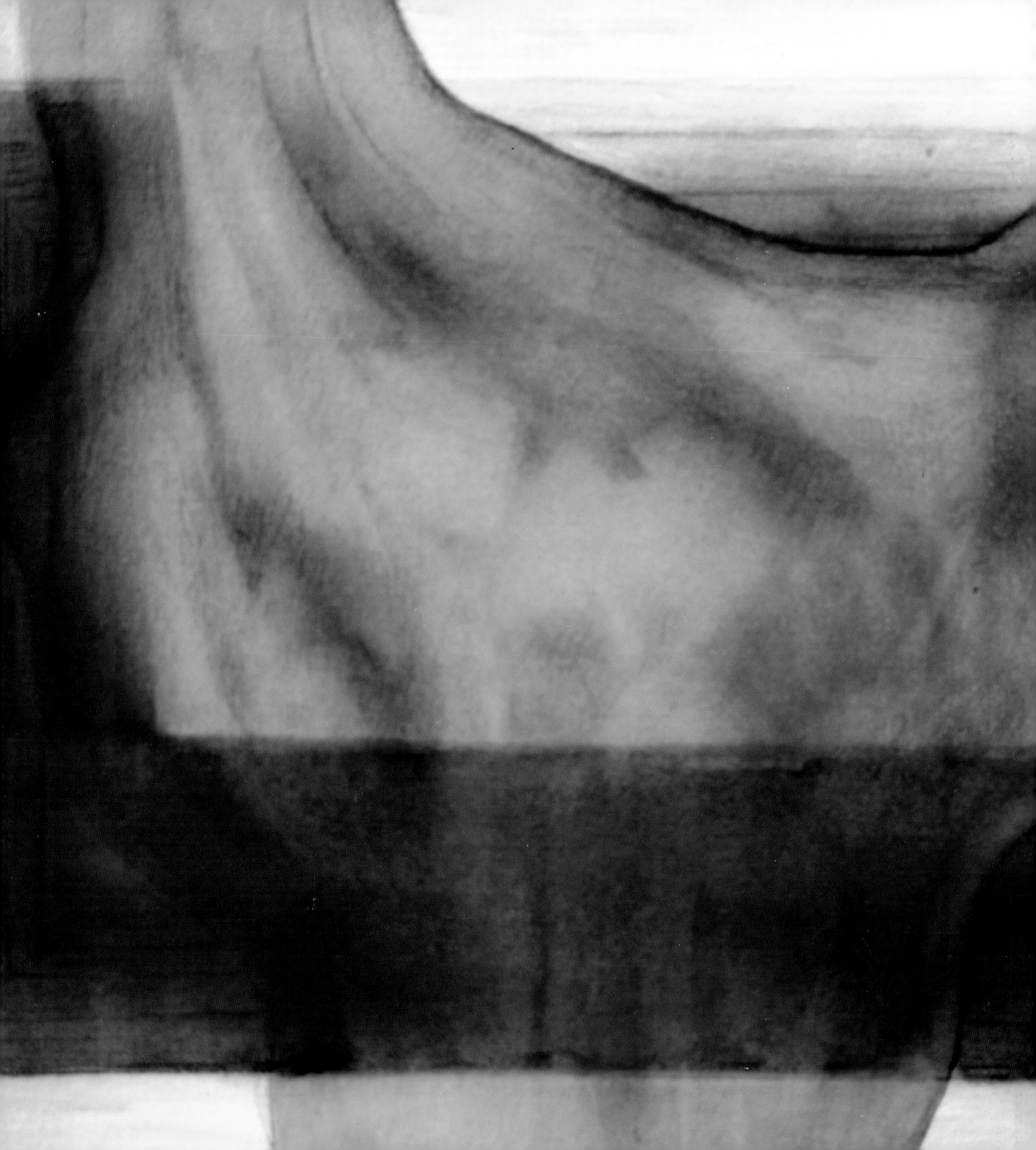